FRANKiE SPARKS

AND THE LUCKY CHARM

FRANKIE SPARKS, THIRD-GRADE INVENTOR

FRANKIE SPARKS
AND THE LUCKY CHARM

BOOK 4

BY MEGAN FRAZER BLAKEMORE
ILLUSTRATED BY NADJA SARELL

ALADDIN   NEW YORK LONDON TORONTO SYDNEY NEW DELHI

ALADDIN

An imprint of Simon & Schuster Children's Publishing Division
1230 Avenue of the Americas, New York, New York 10020
First Aladdin hardcover edition February 2020
Text copyright © 2020 by Megan Frazer Blakemore
Illustrations copyright © 2020 by Nadja Sarell
Hand-lettering design copyright © 2020 by Angela Navarra
Also available in an Aladdin paperback edition
All rights reserved, including the right of reproduction in whole or in part in any form.
ALADDIN and related logo are registered trademarks of Simon & Schuster, Inc.
For information about special discounts for bulk purchases, please contact
Simon & Schuster Special Sales at 1-866-506-1949 or business@simonandschuster.com.
The Simon & Schuster Speakers Bureau can bring authors to your live event.
For more information or to book an event contact the Simon & Schuster Speakers Bureau
at 1-866-248-3049 or visit our website at www.simonspeakers.com.
Series art directed by Laura Lyn DiSiena
Interior designed by Tiara Iandiorio
The illustrations for this book were rendered in pencil line on paper and digital flat tones.
The text of this book was set in Nunito.
Manufactured in the United States of America 0120 FFG
10 9 8 7 6 5 4 3 2 1
Library of Congress Control Number 2019948369
ISBN 978-1-5344-3053-2 (hc)
ISBN 978-1-5344-3052-5 (pbk)
ISBN 978-1-5344-3054-9 (eBook)

For Judith Kurtz,
creator of the original
Wonder Wall

CONTENTS

FRANKiE SPARKS AND THE LUCKY CHARM

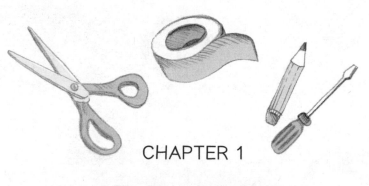

CHAPTER 1

Dog Tricks

ARF! ARF!

When Frankie Sparks heard the dog, she smiled. She walked to Maya's house and into the backyard. Maya's dog, Opus, bounded around on the lawn. When he saw her, he barreled toward her and almost knocked her over.

"I'm teaching him to do tricks!" Maya explained. She stood in the center of the yard, holding a Hula-Hoop.

"Is the trick to knock down your best friend?" Frankie asked with a laugh.

Frankie and Maya had been best friends forever, and Frankie loved Maya's dog almost as much as she loved her own pet, a rat named Buttercup. Opus stopped and gave Frankie a good sniff before starting to sprint again.

"He's supposed to jump through the hoop," Maya said with a shrug. "But mostly he runs around me and around in the yard."

Frankie called Opus to her. He skidded to a stop at her side. "Maybe if you hold the hoop, and I call him from the other side, he'll jump through it." She told Opus to stay and then crossed Maya's lawn so that Maya and the hoop were between her and Opus. It was early spring, and the ground beneath her feet was squishy soft.

"Ready?" Frankie asked Maya.

Maya nodded.

"Here, Opus! Here, boy!" Frankie called.

Opus's ears pricked up. *Arf!* He ran toward Frankie. Frankie clapped and called him again. She was certain Opus was going to jump right through the hoop.

Faster and faster Opus ran, right up to the hoop, and then—*swish*—Opus veered to the right, ran around the hoop, and then turned back toward Frankie. "No, Opus!" Frankie said. "Not like that."

"He's been doing that all afternoon. Just when I think he's going to do it—boom! He goes off in the other direction."

This sounded like a challenge, and there were few things that Frankie liked more than a challenge. "Hmm," she said. "Maybe if I were a little closer to the hoop."

They tried again with Frankie standing closer to the hoop. Opus ran and ran and . . . skidded right under the hoop.

"No, Opus," Maya moaned.

Opus looked back at them with a confused expression on his face.

"It's okay," Frankie said. "You're a good dog." She turned to Maya. "He just doesn't know what we want him to do."

"Let's show him, then!" Maya said with a giggle.

Oh no. Frankie knew where this was going.

"Come on, Frankie!" Maya called. "Go through the hoop!"

"Woof!" Frankie said. She jogged up to the hoop and stepped through.

"Good girl!" Maya said, and patted her on the head.

Arf! Opus said.

But when they called him through again, he just went around the girls. He sat down behind them. *Arf!*

"Opus!" The girls laughed.

Then Frankie snapped her fingers. "I've got it!" It really felt like a light bulb turning on when she got a good idea. Sometimes the light came on all at once, as if with a flick of a switch. Other times it was more like someone was turning up the light slowly, slowly, slowly. This idea came on all at once. "Hold the hoop on the ground," she said. "Then he can just walk right through. Then you can slowly raise it up until he's jumping through."

"Brilliant!" Maya said.

"Brilliant" was just about Frankie's favorite word.

Opus, though, had other ideas. When he got to the hoop, he barked at it; then he took off on his sprint around and around in the yard.

"I guess old dogs really can't be taught new tricks," Frankie said.

"It was a great idea, though," Maya told her.

They watched Opus go around and around. Then, all of a sudden, he dashed toward the garden shed in the back corner of the yard. He pressed his nose into the ground.

Arf-arf! Arf, arf, arf, arf, arf!

"What is he barking at?" Frankie asked.

"Oh, that's our leprechaun hole," Maya explained.

Frankie laughed. *Maya must be joking,* she thought. Everyone knew there was no such thing as a leprechaun.

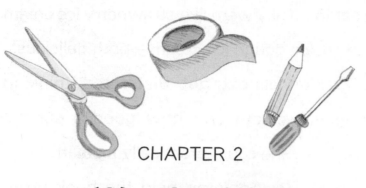

CHAPTER 2

Wonder Wall

MS. APPLETON ROCKED HERSELF IN the chair in the reading nook in the library. Frankie settled back against the risers, already feeling the sweet, dozy sensation that she got when Ms. Appleton read. Even when it was a funny story, Frankie still felt at peace when someone read aloud to her. It was her favorite part of the school day. Her favorite thing to do was invent, but listening to stories was pretty great too. They were like strawberry ice cream and cookie dough ice cream—both delicious.

Frankie almost got distracted thinking about ice cream and how good a sundae would be. She could practically taste it!

Then Ms. Appleton held the book up to her nose and gave it a good sniff. "Smells like adventure!" she announced. She leaned forward and gave her head a good shake, making her curls jump.

She opened up to the first page of the book and read the title: *The Wee Lad and the Not-So-Lucky Leprechaun.* "This, my friends, is a fairy tale. And, like most fairy tales, it begins 'Once upon a time.'"

Frankie quite liked the story. The boy in the book wanted to catch the leprechaun to get its gold, but the leprechaun kept playing tricks on him. There was even a scene where the two of them got caught in a barrel and tumbled down the cliffs right into the ocean, where a whale scooped them up. The boy never got the leprechaun, of course, but it was a funny book all the same.

When it was time to look for books to check out, Frankie said to Maya, "Too bad leprechauns aren't real. I would like to find a pot of gold someday."

Maya's eyebrows jumped up underneath her bangs.

Ravi asked, "What would you do with all that gold?"

"I could buy so many tools and materials. I could invent just about anything. I bet I could even figure out how to make a real, working hover board!" Frankie exclaimed.

"They *are* real," Maya said.

"Hover boards?" Frankie asked. "There are some pretty close ones, but not a real, legit hover board."

"No," Maya said. "Leprechauns. I told you. One lives under our shed. Or maybe it's a gnome. We're not quite sure."

Frankie felt her eyes go wide. "You were serious about that?" Frankie asked. "I thought you were joking." Her best friend couldn't possibly believe in mythical creatures!

"Yes, I am serious. We have a leprechaun living in our yard."

Frankie shook her head. "That's ridiculous. It's probably an opossum or a skunk or something."

"I'm not being ridiculous," Maya insisted. "Matt and I saw his footprints. Little feet, like humans have, but with only four toes."

"No way," Frankie said.

"Yes way," Maya said. She led Frankie into the story area, where Ms. Appleton had left her book. Maya pointed to the label on the spine. "See, it has numbers on it."

Ms. Appleton had taught them that the nonfiction books in the library always had call numbers on them.

Maya read out the numbers: "'Three ninety-eight point two.'"

"Are you looking for more books on leprechauns?" Ms. Appleton asked.

Maya shook her head. "I'm proving to Frankie that leprechauns are real," Maya said.

"Because they're in the nonfiction section."

Ms. Appleton smiled. "I'm afraid it's not quite as simple as that. I guess I should have been clearer. There's actually a Dewey decimal number for fiction. We just put leprechaun books in their own section to make it easier for you to find what you're looking for. That call number—three ninety-eight point two—that's for fairy tales."

"Ha!" Frankie said. "So they are not true."

"Well," Ms. Appleton said, "I wouldn't necessarily say that."

"So leprechauns are real?" Maya asked.

"I wouldn't say that, either."

"What would you say?"

Ms. Appleton pointed to the big bulletin board in the library. The words "I wonder" were cut out, letter by letter, and stapled to the bright blue background. Kids could write things that they wondered about on slips of paper and stick them to the wall. Then, if you had time after doing the library activities, you could pick an "I wonder" and try to answer

it. It could be your own wondering or some-one else's. Frankie had already answered two: *I wonder why pumping on the swing makes you go higher* and *I wonder who invented the toilet.* She knew that Luke had written the second one as a joke, but Ms. Appleton had taken it seriously, and so had Frankie.

Now Ms. Appleton looked at Frankie and Maya. "I think it's a great 'I wonder,' don't you?"

"I do," Maya said. She took a black marker and wrote on a green square of paper in her neat handwriting: *I wonder if leprechauns are real.* She used a thumbtack to pin it to the bright blue paper.

Before Frankie could say anything, Ms. Cupid, their teacher, asked them to check out their books and get ready to go. Frankie quickly found a book about internal combustion engines to check out.

"I'm looking for a straight, quiet line," Ms. Cupid said. Frankie zipped her lips. Sometimes Ms. Cupid chose a mystery walker, and if that person was quiet the entire walk back to class, they would get a special prize. Frankie had never been the mystery walker, but she desperately wanted to be. Or, she worried, maybe she had been, but she had been chatty and so she hadn't gotten her prize. She didn't mean to be chatty. She just had so much on her mind and so much to share.

This time she was quiet the whole way.

And of course Lila Jones was the mystery walker. Lila chose a sticker of a glittery mermaid with googly eyes that wiggled back and forth when Lila shook the sticker. Lila put it right into her pencil case, where no one else could see it.

Frankie was fuming and had nearly forgotten all about leprechauns, but then she remembered the words on the paper—*I wonder if leprechauns are real*—and she knew right then that this was going to be the third wonder she solved.

CHAPTER 3

Science to
the Rescue

ALL DAY LONG FRANKIE'S BRAIN SPUN.
She felt like she had a washing machine in her
head, stirring her thoughts back and forth and
round and round. If leprechauns were real, she
reasoned, surely someone would have seen one.
Surely someone would have caught one by now.

On the other hand, there were lots of things
that people hadn't understood at first, and

then science had figured them out. Like the giant squid. When people first saw them in the ocean, people thought they were sea monsters or maybe mermen. Later, scientists identified them by their remains as real animals, but it wasn't until decades later that someone got a picture of one. Maybe leprechauns were as hard to find as giant squid.

Frankie thought about it as she ate her applesauce at lunch; she thought about it while Ms. Cupid read aloud; she thought about it while they were supposed to be working on their math facts.

By the end of the day, her brain was exhausted.

She took the bus to her father's nursery. He had the place decorated for Saint Patrick's Day, with pots of clover out front and a cutout of a leprechaun in the window. On his message board he'd slid in the letters to say:

CAPTURE THE LUCK OF THE IRISH

GET YOUR GREEN TODAY!

While her father helped a customer pick out the best kind of roses for her garden, Frankie perched on a stool behind the counter.

She was helping her dad by organizing seed packets. Her dad had once told her that seeds had been at the start of figuring out genetics—how parents pass along traits like hair color to their kids. Frankie guessed that genetics was another thing that people had wondered about until a scientist had stepped in and figured it out.

A light bulb went off above her head. The light-bulb feeling was much more common for Frankie, and much more pleasant, than washing-machine brain. She was an inventor, which was a kind of scientist. She had a question in front of her, and she needed to use science to find the answer. She took out a piece of paper. *Do leprakans exist?* she wrote. *Prove or disprove.*

Then she stared at the paper. She stared at it some more.

Maybe this wasn't going to be so easy after all.

Her dad came back to the counter and saw her staring at the paper. "'Do leprechauns exist?'" he read over her shoulder. "That's an age-old question."

"I'm going to answer it," Frankie said. "I think."

"What's your hypothesis?" he asked.

Frankie nodded. A hypothesis was like a prediction for how you thought an experiment would turn out—your educated guess about how things would work, before you investigated them. "My hypothesis is that they don't exist," Frankie said.

"I see," he said. "And how do you plan to test your hypothesis?"

Frankie slumped. That was her exact problem. She didn't know how to test her hypothesis. There were lots of ways to prove something *did* exist, but how did you prove that something *didn't* exist?

"Ah, I see," her dad said. "Listen, I've known you a long time."

Frankie put her chin on the counter, but lifted her head to look at her dad. "My whole life, practically," she said.

"Your whole life exactly," he responded. "And here's what I know about you: When you have a problem, you figure it out. This one might seem like a tough challenge, but I have faith in you." He reached out and tousled her curls.

"Thanks, Dad," she said.

He picked up a small potted fern. "Just don't count on a trip to Ireland, okay?" he said with a laugh before making his way back out into the aisles of the greenhouse.

Frankie knew that she couldn't go all the way to Ireland, but her dad had given her a good idea. She should write down everything she knew about leprechauns. She took her little red inventing-and-ideas notebook out of her backpack. She started her list with where lep-rechauns lived:

- *They come from Ireland*
- *They like green places—lots of trees and grass and stuff*

Frankie looked around. There weren't many places that had more green than her dad's nursery, and she had never in her life seen any evidence of a leprechaun there. That seemed like proof that they didn't exist. Then again, Maya's lawn was greener than just about any other lawn that Frankie had ever seen. So, if leprechauns *did* exist, Maya's backyard would be a place that they'd like.

Frankie kept writing. Most of the ideas she wrote down came from the book that Ms. Appleton had read, but others came from TV shows or other stories she had heard. She added idea after idea until she had almost the whole page filled up.

- *They are small*
- *They wear green*
- *They like gold*
- *They are triky*

- *They are smart*

- *Most have beerds*

- *Job: fixing shoes*

- *Hobby: hiding gold at the end of the rainbow*

When she was done, she looked at her notes. Pretty impressive! She wasn't sure if she had spelled all the words correctly, but that was okay. The problem was, she wasn't any closer to figuring out how to prove that leprechauns didn't exist. Proving they *did* exist would be easy. She would just need to catch one. But she was still stuck with the same question: How do you prove that something *doesn't* exist?

And then it hit her! If you could prove a leprechaun existed by catching one, then you proved one didn't exist by *not* catching one.

She had to make a trap. Not just a regular leprechaun trap. She had to make the most amazing leprechaun trap ever. And when that amazing, stupendous, magnificent leprechaun trap didn't catch a single leprechaun, that would prove that they were not real.

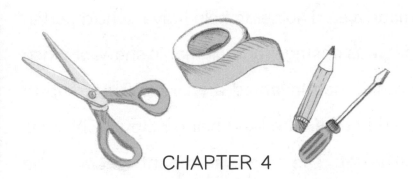

CHAPTER 4

The Perfect Trap

THE NEXT MORNING WAS A SATURDAY.
Frankie got up early and went to her invention
lab. It had been a closet, but her parents had
helped her convert it into her own special space
for designing and building her inventions. She
rolled her chair out from under the desk, sat on
it, and started slowly spinning herself around.

Normally, when she invented, she was
inventing to help someone. Like when she'd

made a card holder to help Maya, who'd gotten nervous onstage for their magic show, or when Frankie had invented a way for Buttercup to feed herself. She liked being helpful. This was different. The trap was meant to catch the leprechaun. It was *for* a leprechaun, but it wasn't meant to help it. Frankie would have felt a little bit bad about that if she had thought that leprechauns were real.

When she invented for people, she thought about what that person liked and what that person needed. She took out her inventing-and-ideas notebook, opened to the list of things she knew about leprechauns, and read it over. Some of the details were more impor-tant than others. She circled the facts that she thought were most important.

*They come from Ireland
* They like green places
    —Lots of trees and grass
       and stuff
* They are small
* They wear green
* They like =GOLD=
* They are triky
* They are smart
* most have beerds
* JOB: fixing shoes
* HOBBY: hiding gold at the <u>end</u>
    of the Rainbow

X

When she was designing the trap, she would need to think about these things and incorporate them into her design.

Next she decided to think about what she knew about traps. She drew a picture of a box with a stick holding it up. The stick had a string attached to it. Under the box was a treat. She had seen this kind of trap in cartoons. When the bunny or whatever went to get the treat, the person pulled the string, and the stick fell down. The box fell too, and trapped the bunny. That was how the trap was supposed to work, anyway. Sometimes in the cartoons she watched, things got a little silly.

From her drawing she knew that she needed three things for her trap. She wrote these down in her notebook as well:

1. *Some sort of bait to attract the leprechaun*
2. *Something to set off the trap*

3. Something to make sure the

leprechaun can't get out once

the trap goes off

The obvious choice for bait was gold, but she didn't have any gold. She wondered if leprechauns liked pennies. She had lots of those. She kept them in her piggy bank by her bed. Every time she found one, she dropped it in. When she had enough, she was going to buy a soldering iron, a special tool for connecting things, like in electronics. It was almost as useful as duct tape! Aunt Nichelle, who worked as an engineer, said she'd teach Frankie how to use it. Then Frankie could hook up wires and batteries and lights and stuff. It was hard to save money, especially when Wink's Magic and Games Emporium sold such cool magic tricks, but she was doing her best.

Anyway, she didn't want to lose her pennies, but since leprechauns weren't real, that wasn't really a risk. She would plan on using pennies for bait unless she thought of something better. The other two parts of the trap were the bigger challenges. How big did the trap need to be? She knew leprechauns were small, but how small? It wasn't like anyone had ever measured one!

Frankie remembered the so-called leprechaun hole under the shed at Maya's house. Frankie was able to see maybe six inches into the hole. So Frankie decided that the leprechaun mustn't be any taller than six inches. She wrote that down on her paper.

Now she knew that the trap had to be bigger than six inches in any direction.

Finally, the hardest part. Leprechauns were smart. They wouldn't fall for any old box and stick. She needed something much more clever. Luckily, Frankie was pretty smart too.

She closed her eyes and took a deep breath in. When she opened her eyes, she grabbed a new piece of paper and began to draw.

When she finished, she clapped her hands together.

She had drawn a treasure chest with its lid open. A small cauldron hung from the top of the chest, filled with gold coins. The cauldron rested on top of what looked like clouds. This was the genius of the trap.

She would put a layer of cotton across the top of the chest. It would be stiff enough to stay in place, and even to have the cauldron touch it. But as soon as someone—like a leprechaun—stepped onto it, he would fall right through. The pennies were her bait. And the cauldron would be what caused the top to drop and trap the leprechaun inside. She had met all three of her requirements. Perfect!

Frankie bit her lip. Well, maybe not quite perfect. She didn't believe in leprechauns, that was true, but on the one-in-a-million chance that they were real and she caught one, she didn't want it to get hurt. Plus, an animal might get into the trap by accident. Frankie would add more cotton to the bottom of the box so that whatever landed in it would have a safe, soft landing. She'd add a small dish for water, too. Now the design was perfect! All she had to do was *not* catch a leprechaun.

CHAPTER 5

Watching
and Waiting

"TA-DA!" FRANKIE ANNOUNCED WHEN
Maya opened her front door.

"Hi, Frankie!" Maya said.

"I came right over when I finished." She
carefully held out her invention to Maya. "It's a
leprechaun trap!"

Maya regarded it skeptically. "That's going
to catch the leprechaun?"

Frankie opened up the box and explained how it worked.

"So the leprechaun falls down into the box and then is stuck there?" Maya asked, her doubt turning to excitement.

"Precisely," Frankie said. "Pretty genius, right?"

"It's fantastic! Let's go try it out."

The two girls went around the house to the backyard, their feet squishing in the fresh grass.

Frankie regarded the hole under the shed. "Let's see," she said. "We don't want to be too obvious. If we put the trap right by the hole, he'll surely suspect something. That is, he *would* suspect something, *if* leprechauns were real."

"Maybe we shouldn't talk about it right in

front of the hole," Maya said. "He might never come out again."

Frankie knew that the leprechaun could hear them only if he had real ears, which he didn't, because he wasn't real at all, but she whispered, "Good point. How about over here?"

A lilac bush was just starting to bud at the edge of Maya's lawn. Frankie placed the box under the lowest branches and carefully opened the lid. She made sure that the pennies were in the cauldron and that the cotton batting was placed just so. The trap was perfect. She almost wished leprechauns *were* real, because her trap would surely catch one!

"Now what?" Maya whispered.

"We wait," Frankie said. "But not too close."

The two girls tiptoed across the lawn.

"What are you two up to?" Maya's brother, Matt, yelled from the back porch.

"Shh!" Maya yelled. "You'll scare it away."

"*You'll* scare it away!" Frankie whisper-yelled at Maya.

"Scare what away?" Matt asked.

Frankie and Maya both waved their hands frantically, trying to tell him to be quiet.

"What?" he yelled again.

"The leprechaun!" Maya finally said, as softly as she could. "We're going to catch it."

Matt snorted. "You two? Catch a leprechaun?"

"Would you stop yelling about it?" Frankie told him.

"Yeah! If he hears, he'll never come out," Maya added.

The two girls stood with their hands on their hips, glaring at Matt.

"Okay, okay," he said, holding up his hands. "I just think you two have no idea what you're getting into, trying to catch a lep—"

"Matt!" Maya said.

"Trying to do you-know-what to you-know-who," Matt said. "They're tricky, and a lot smarter than you."

"No one's smarter than Frankie Sparks," Frankie said, puffing out her chest. "Or Maya," she added quickly.

"Yeah!" Maya said.

"Well, if you're so smart, how come Opus is licking your trap?" Matt asked.

"What?" Frankie exclaimed. She and Maya ran over to the dog while Matt laughed.

"No!" Maya said. "Not for you!"

If dogs could shrug, then Opus would have shrugged. He pressed his head against Frankie's hand so that she would pet him. The two girls and the dog went back across the lawn and sat under the old oak tree. They could see the trap and the hole, but they were far enough away, they thought, that the leprechaun wouldn't be bothered by them. If he saw them, he would probably just think they were having a picnic or looking at clouds or counting acorns, all the things they normally did in Maya's backyard.

They watched and they waited.

They waited and they watched.

They waited. They watched.

Nothing happened.

"Are leprechauns nocturnal?" Maya asked.

"No. They come out for rainbows," Frankie said. "So they must be out during the day, not the nighttime."

"Good point."

They watched and waited some more.

When a whole hour had passed, Maya said, "I'm hungry. And my mom made double fudge brownies. Let's go inside and have a snack."

Frankie was also feeling pretty hungry. "Okay," she said. "I mean, if leprechauns are real, we don't have to see it get trapped, right? It will just get trapped."

"Right, we don't have to sit around and wait."

The two friends went inside and ate double fudge brownies and drank milk. Then they decided to play a game of checkers. Then they put on their magic-show costumes and pretended they were part of a traveling circus and talked to each other with made-up accents.

Another hour went by before they decided to check on the trap again.

They crept up to the lilac bush.

The leprechaun trap was untouched.

"Just as I thought!" Frankie said. "There's your proof. I made a perfect leprechaun trap, and no leprechaun was caught."

Maya crouched down low. "What's that?" she asked, pointing at little divots in the grass.

"Just little bumps," Frankie said. "Like from the rain or something."

"It didn't rain. I think they look like footprints," Maya said. "They seem a little green to me."

"Maya!" Frankie said, exasperated. "You said yourself the trap was fantastic."

"Sure," Maya said. "But what I'm realizing is that just because your trap didn't catch a leprechaun, that doesn't mean they don't exist. The only way to be sure would be if you had a foolproof trap. Especially when it comes to leprechauns. They're tricky. They're all about fooling."

"It *is* a foolproof trap."

"Are you sure?" Maya asked.

Frankie was about to say yes, but then she realized that she wasn't absolutely, positively, no doubt about it, 100 percent sure. "No," she admitted. "But I will be. If I prove to you that this is a foolproof trap, will you believe me that leprechauns aren't real?"

Maya thought about this for a second. She didn't take such types of deals lightly. "Yes," she said. "I will."

She reached out her hand, and the two girls shook on it.

Now all Frankie had to do was prove that her trap was foolproof. Easy-peasy, right? Frankie wasn't so sure.

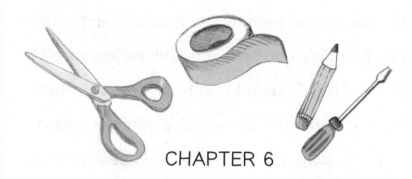

CHAPTER 6

Expert Engineer

FRANKIE'S EYES GREW WIDE AS AUNT Nichelle placed a huge slice of lemon meringue pie in front of her. The way the meringue was piled up seemed to defy gravity. Of course, if anyone could defy gravity with a pie or anything else, it was Frankie's aunt Nichelle. She was a rocket scientist—and a really great baker.

They were finishing up their Sunday dinner. Once a month Frankie's family went over to have dinner with her aunt, uncle, and cousins. Frankie's cousins were still babies, pretty much. Frankie didn't mind playing with them for a little bit, but she much preferred spending time with Aunt Nichelle and hearing what she was working on.

All through dinner Frankie had been thinking about how she could prove her trap was foolproof. Now, though, her brain was finally distracted. She scooped up a bite of pie and let it dissolve in her mouth. Delicious! It was like taking a bite of the summer that was on its way.

"Good?" Frankie's uncle Charlie chuckled.

"Mm-hmm." Frankie nodded, her mouth too full of pie to say a real word.

"Well, finish up, because after dinner I need

a young inventor to help me with a problem," Aunt Nichelle said.

Frankie ate so fast that the pie disappeared like in one of her magic tricks.

Aunt Nichelle brought Frankie into her home office. "Some of my colleagues are working on space gardens," Aunt Nichelle said. "We want to be able to grow food up in space so that the astronauts can have fresh fruit and vegetables."

"That's cool!" Frankie said. "They'll still get space ice cream, though, right?"

"If they want it," Aunt Nichelle said, wrinkling her nose. Frankie loved space ice cream, which was basically a block of ice cream–flavored foam that melted in your mouth. Aunt Nichelle called it an insult to taste buds.

"They've had a lot of luck with greens, and potatoes seem to be doing well. Now they're working on juicier vegetables."

Aunt Nichelle called up a file on her computer. She showed Frankie pictures of the space gardens, where different types of lettuce grew. The soil was all contained in boxes so it wouldn't fly around in the outer-space greenhouse. The water was piped right into the boxes too.

Then Aunt Nichelle showed her a video of a tomato bursting in a zero-gravity environment. The goo and seeds from inside went everywhere. "You see the problem?" Aunt Nichelle asked.

"What a mess! Can't they put a box around it like they do for the soil and water? That way if one tomato breaks, it will be contained," Frankie said.

"Smart girl!" Aunt Nichelle replied. "That's what they've been trying. It seems to work pretty well. They're figuring out a way to clean out the box so that when they open it, any mess doesn't fly out. After all, each tomato plant produces many tomatoes, and our workers don't want to give up on a whole plant just because one tomato explodes."

Frankie nodded. "So what do you need my help with?"

"I need you to tell me all the ways a tomato might break."

Frankie thought about this for a second. Sometimes she helped in her dad's nursery, so she knew a lot about plants. The tomato plants were some of her favorites because they smelled—and tasted—so good. "Sometimes the tomatoes get too heavy and the stem breaks. Sometimes they just grow with cracks in them. Sometimes people bump them. Little kids like to squeeze them—not like there would be a lot of kids in space. Or animals. They steal them sometimes and make a mess."

"Good list," Aunt Nichelle said. "Anything else? Think big. Think wild!"

Aunt Nichelle always told her to "think wild," because sometimes in the wildness there was a good idea. "Well, here on Earth, a hurricane could knock them down. Or an earthquake. So, I guess . . . Wait. Is there turbulence in space? If there is, then that could knock the tomatoes off the vines. And then they'd fall—" She stopped herself. "Well, they wouldn't fall; they would float up and then hit the roof of the box and maybe break."

Aunt Nichelle laughed. "Now you've got your thinking cap on." She was writing down everything Frankie said.

"Do you think the lack of gravity could make them burst somehow?" Frankie asked. "Like maybe they would grow differently or something?"

"We're definitely looking into that."

"Why do you want to know all the ways that a tomato might break, anyway?"

"Well, when you're inventing something, it's a good idea to think of all the ways that things might go wrong. You want to identify all the possible ways that your invention might fail, and then you can address those possibilities."

Frankie thought about this for a minute. "Like trial and error?"

"Exactly," Aunt Nichelle said. "But in this method you're anticipating the errors, not waiting for them to just happen."

Frankie thought some more. "That's what I need to do with my leprechaun trap!" she exclaimed.

"Your what?" Aunt Nichelle asked.

Frankie explained about the trap and how Maya wanted proof that the trap hadn't failed. "I need to anticipate all the ways it could fail, and improve my design so that my trap is undoubtable."

Aunt Nichelle grinned and tapped Frankie on the nose. "That's why, my dear, you are my favorite inventor. Now let your creativity run wild and come up with all the ways that leprechaun trap might fail."

To let her creativity run wild was not something Frankie needed to be told twice. It was how her brain operated most of the time. However, it was time to go home and go to bed. Her brainstorm would have to wait until the next day.

CHAPTER 7

The Pang

IN ART CLASS FRANKIE DREW LEPRE-
chauns and leprechaun traps. Just like Aunt
Nichelle had told her, she let her mind go wild,
imagining all the possible ways a leprechaun
could escape her trap.

She drew a little leprechaun using tiny
scissors to cut a hole out of the box. *You
can't catch me!* she wrote in a speech bubble.

Then she drew herself and a thought bubble: *Curses. Foiled again!*

Maya peered over her shoulder. "Whoa! I hadn't thought of that. Do you think leprechauns travel around with tiny scissors?"

"I bet some of them do," Frankie said. "I have to think of every possibility."

Lila Jones, who sat at the art table with them, said, "I bet they have tiny *gold* scissors."

Frankie figured that was probably true, but she never liked to admit when Lila was right. So she colored the scissors in using her pencil.

"What if the leprechaun was an inventor like you, Frankie?" Ravi asked. "He might have tape with him and string and a tiny little notebook to write things down in."

Frankie grinned. "Yeah, and a tool belt, too." She really wanted a tool belt. She was thinking of making one for herself, but she would need to learn how to use the sewing machine. In the meantime, she drew a new leprechaun—a girl—and gave her a tool belt. This one said, *There's no trap I can't outsmart!*

Ms. Burman, the art teacher, came and peered over her shoulder. "I didn't know you were working on a comic." Ms. Burman tapped Frankie's paper. "What happened to your sculpture of Mae Jemison's rocket?"

"I'm taking a break from that," Frankie replied. "This is a new project. An urgent project."

Ms. Burman always let them decide for themselves what they were going to work on.

She talked a lot about the process of making art and how each artist approached each project in a different way, so she let them work at their own pace on their own projects. For Frankie, art was a lot like engineering, so she loved being in Ms. Burman's studio.

"Urgent art?" Ms. Burman asked.

"I designed a leprechaun trap, and now I'm making it foolproof," Frankie said. "These are all the ways it could fail."

Ms. Burman nodded. "You've certainly given a lot of movement to that leprechaun character. And I love your use of color."

"Thanks," Frankie said.

Ms. Burman grinned. Frankie was pretty sure that Ms. Burman had light-bulb moments, just like she did. "I think a really neat project would be to share these drawings along with your trap. It would be a view into the engineer's mind!"

Frankie liked that idea. "Okay! Once I'm done not catching a leprechaun, I'll bring the trap in."

"Not catching?" Ms. Burman asked.

"It's my leprechaun," Maya explained. "But Frankie doesn't believe in it."

"So you're trying to prove it doesn't exist by not catching it?" Ms. Burman asked.

"Correct!" Frankie replied. "That's why the trap needs to be foolproof."

"Well, keep me posted," Ms. Burman said. Then she went over to another table, where Suki was working with William on a model of the Parthenon.

Luke, who was sitting at the table behind

Frankie, leaned back in his chair. "Just stomp on it," he said.

"What?" Frankie asked.

"If you want the trap to fail, stomp on it. If you can stomp on it and it doesn't break, then it's fail-proof." He swung his fist, clutching his paintbrush, down onto the table as he spoke. Little drops of green paint went everywhere.

"It's not that simple," Frankie said. "Even if a leprechaun were big enough to squash it, which it's not—"

"How do you know?" Luke asked.

"I just do. Leprechauns are small," Frankie answered.

"Have you ever seen one?" he asked.

"Of course I haven't," she told him. "They aren't real."

"Then how do you know how big they are?"

This question was a real conundrum. Her mind had just started to spin on it when Lila said, "I believe in leprechauns. And fairies and elves and all of those magical things."

"Not me," Ravi said. He put down his paintbrush. He had been working on a watercolor of the river that flowed through the town. "If they exist, why haven't we seen them? Why is there no evidence?"

"Exactly!" Frankie said.

"Also, rainbows don't really have ends. It's just light going through water droplets. That's why you have to stand in a certain spot to see them. If you tried to move to get to the so-called end, the rainbow would just disappear."

"Exactly!" Frankie said again.

Suki, from her table, said, "I believe in leprechauns. Last Saint Patrick's Day there were little green footprints on our counter."

Luke laughed. "At my house the water in the toilet turned green! I think a leprechaun—"

"Luke," Ms. Burman said from the front of the art studio. Frankie often wondered how teachers were able to hear everything going on in their rooms. Maybe they had some sort of hearing enhancer.

While Frankie wanted to pursue this line of thought and figure out how a teacher might make a secret hearing enhancer, something else was going on. It was in her stomach. She didn't feel sick. Frankie had a pang. She didn't like having pangs, because usually they came when she had done something wrong.

She looked at Maya. Maya was weaving gold and green strips of fabric together. It was, Frankie realized, a leprechaun blanket. The pang got a little sharper. Maya really and truly believed in leprechauns. So did Lila and Suki. Lila might just be saying so to push Frankie's buttons, but Frankie was pretty sure that Suki was telling the truth. And Suki was smart. Could the other girls be right about leprechauns?

Ms. Burman crossed to the center of the room. "I see we've all gone a little wild for leprechauns today," she said. "You know I don't mind when you follow your imaginations, but it can't be a distraction."

Frankie sniffed. She couldn't deny that she was distracted. The pang in her stomach was growing into a knot. But it wasn't a guilty knot, she realized. Those made her feel sad and antsy. This one was a little scarier.

"Let's keep our conversations to our own tables, okay?" Ms. Burman said.

That was fine with Frankie. Everyone jumping in was just making her more confused. On the *Yes, leprechauns are real* side were Maya, Lila, Suki, and Luke. On the *No, leprechauns are not real* side were just her and Ravi. It was true that Ravi was very, very smart. He was also, quite proudly, a cynic, meaning he didn't believe much of anything without proof. Normally that made him a good companion, but . . . Her thoughts trailed off into a tangle.

She sighed.

"What's wrong?" Maya asked.

Frankie, though, turned to Lila. "What makes you so sure that leprechauns are real?" she asked.

Lila, though, just shrugged. "I believe it, that's all. It's nice to believe in things."

This time it was Maya who said, "Exactly."

Frankie's whole stomach dropped. What if she was wrong? What if leprechauns really did exist? Or, what if they didn't exist? What if she was about to ruin something nice for her best friend?

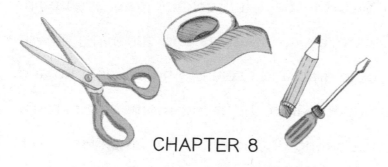

CHAPTER 8

Possible Fails

FRANKIE WAS STUMPED.

She sat at the kitchen table with her leprechaun trap in front of her.

She had so many questions, and not enough answers. What if leprechauns really were real? What if they were just so smart that they'd never been caught? What if everyone else was right, and she was wrong?

She stared at her trap. She used to think

it was the best leprechaun trap ever built. Before, it was sparkles and sunshine; now it looked drab and useless. She picked it up and brought it into the living room. Her parents were sitting on the couch together. Her mom was reading the newspaper, and her dad was reading a book about beekeeping.

Frankie said, "May I present, for the very first time, the world's most amazing leprechaun trap!"

Her mom raised her eyebrows. "Leprechaun trap? Why do you want to catch a leprechaun?"

"I don't!" Frankie said.

Her mom looked confused, but her dad said, "I knew you would figure it out. Frankie is trying to prove that leprechauns don't exist, so she made a trap to catch one."

"And when I don't catch one," Frankie added, "even with the world's most amazing leprechaun trap ever, then that will be proof that they don't exist. At least that was the plan."

"And now?"

"Now I'm starting to worry. Almost everyone at school thinks leprechauns are real. I'm starting to have doubts."

"So now you think they might be real after all?" her dad asked.

Frankie nodded glumly.

"I'm not sure how that changes anything," her mom said.

"It doesn't?"

"You made the trap to prove that leprechauns didn't exist, right? You had a theory that they were just fantasy. Now you have a question: 'Are leprechauns real?'" her mom explained.

Frankie could see where her mom was going with this. Either way, the trap would answer the question. As long as it worked.

Her mom picked up the trap. "So you've brainstormed, designed, and built. Have you tested it yet?"

"We tried it at Maya's, but we didn't catch anything," Frankie told her.

"That's your first piece of evidence."

Frankie nodded.

"What happened with the trap at Maya's?" her mom asked. "Anything notable?"

"Opus was interested in it," Frankie said.

"Well, that's good news," her dad said.

"One creature is attracted to your trap, so probably others would be too."

"Although," her mom mused, "that might actually be a problem. You want to catch a leprechaun, not a squirrel."

"I guess that's another way it could fail," Frankie said. She explained what Aunt Nichelle had said about anticipating failure, and Frankie told them about all the work she had done in art class.

Frankie's mom shook her head. Frankie felt that pang again. Was her mom disappointed in her now too?

"What?" Frankie asked.

"Why are you so down in the dumps, Frankie?"

"I told you, I—"

But her mom stopped her by shaking her head again. She said, "You've identified your problem: You want to know if leprechauns exist or not. You've made a plan: Identify all the possible ways the trap could fail, and fix them. You're not stuck, Frankie. You're ready to roll." Her mom paused. "But you don't look ready to roll."

Frankie slumped down onto the couch between her parents. "Maya really, really believes in leprechauns. If I prove they don't exist, I think she'll be sad."

"That's a different kind of problem," her mom said.

Her dad put his hand on her knee. "Maya is in on the plan, right?"

Frankie nodded.

"Well, then I think you need to trust Maya," her dad said. "You may be disappointed to be wrong, but finding out one way or the other is more important to you, right?"

"Uh-huh," Frankie said.

"Maya wants to know too," her mom said. "And she must know that she could wind up sad about the outcome."

"But maybe ask her one more time, just to be sure," Frankie's mom continued. "After you've perfected your trap, of course."

Frankie smiled. Her parents were right.

She took the leprechaun trap back from her mom and hurried to her lab. In her invention notebook she wrote down all the ways she had thought of that her trap could fail. One by one she solved them.

Possible fail # 1: Leprechaun might have tiny scissors. She searched through her recycled materials bin until she found a plastic box from the baby spinach her dad liked. The shell box fit inside her leprechaun trap with just a little room to spare. She filled that extra space with sand. Now, even if the leprechaun had sharp enough scissors to cut the plastic, the sand would spin in around him.

She felt her heart soar a little.

Possible fail # 2: Subject can reach cauldron and remove bait without stepping on clouds.

Frankie took the cauldron out. She shortened the string that held the cauldron up and removed some of the pennies so that the leprechaun would need to reach in deeper to get the bait.

She kept going and going, and as she

solved each possible problem, she hummed a little song to herself.

Possible fail #7: Animals attracted to trap.

. . .

Possible fail #13: Leprechaun is able to climb walls and push open lid.

. . .

Possible fail #17: Some other way the leprechaun manages to get out.

Frankie realized that even with her great big brain, she might not be able to think of everything. She needed a way to make sure that if a leprechaun *did* manage to break out of the trap, there would be evidence of it. She took down her super special inventing tool, the one she reserved for only the most important inventions: glitter.

Glitter was beautiful, but one sprinkle, and you'd find it everywhere for days. Ms. Cupid didn't allow it in her classroom, and Ms. Burman made you fill out an application to use it.

Frankie unscrewed the glitter cap and

sprinkled the glitter all along the bottom of the box. If a leprechaun escaped her trap, he would leave a trail of glitter behind him.

"Wait!" Frankie said out loud. "One more thing!" She ran up to her bedroom, and nearly tripped over piles of books and dirty clothes. She dug through a box on her bedside table. "Aha!" She'd found just what she was looking for—the rainbow necklace charm she had won at last year's spring fair. She brought it back down and glued it to the top of the box. Every good leprechaun trap needed a lucky charm, she thought.

Now she had a truly foolproof trap. Amazing!

It was time to bring it back to Maya's.

CHAPTER 9

Catching a Leprechaun

ARF! OPUS BARKED WHEN FRANKIE came into the backyard. Maya was back to trying to teach her dog tricks. This time she was trying to get him to roll over.

"Is that the trap?" Maya asked.

"Yep! New and improved. Now we'll know for sure whether or not there are leprechauns."

"I like the little rainbow," Maya said.

"That's the lucky charm," Frankie explained. "Even science needs a little luck from time to time."

Together the girls set up the trap, and then they went onto Maya's back porch to watch and wait. They were quiet. Maybe a little too quiet.

"Maya," Frankie said. "Are you mad that I don't believe in leprechauns?"

"No," Maya said. "Not mad, really. You're just so sure about everything."

Frankie was confused. Maya was saying that like it was a bad thing. Still, Frankie admitted, "I'm not so sure about leprechauns anymore. You, Lila, Suki, and Luke all believe in them."

Maya laughed.

"What?" Frankie asked.

"Well, while you were starting to wonder if they were real, I was starting to think they were make-believe."

That *was* pretty funny, Frankie thought.

"But do you really want to know the truth?" Frankie asked. "Even if they might not be real?"

Maya nodded. "Do you really want to

know?" Maya asked. "Even if they might be?"

"If my trap caught a real-life leprechaun—well, then that would prove that I'm the world's greatest inventor!"

They left the trap there for three days. Each day Frankie checked in with Maya. They inspected the trap. Everything worked just the way it was supposed to, but no leprechaun and no glitter trail.

On the third day, Frankie crouched down next to the trap. She inspected it on all sides. No damage. No glitter. No leprechaun. A grin spread over her face. "We did it!" she said. "I made a foolproof trap, and it didn't catch a leprechaun. So now we can say for sure that they don't exist." She held up her hand to Maya for a high five.

Maya, though, shook her head. "I still don't think we can, Frankie." She picked up the trap. "You made an amazing trap. The best one ever. If there were a trap that was going to catch a leprechaun, it would be this one."

"Yeah?" Frankie prompted.

"Just because it didn't catch a leprechaun doesn't mean they aren't real."

"But that was our plan," Frankie said.

"I know," Maya said. She looked about as disappointed as Frankie felt. "Remember when we were trying to get Opus to go through the hoop?"

Frankie nodded. "He went every which way but through."

"Right. We had the hoop. Opus just wouldn't jump through it."

"So you're saying that we had the trap, but the leprechaun just didn't come to it?"

Maya nodded. "It's okay, Frankie," Maya said. She handed Frankie the trap. "You did your best."

It didn't feel like doing her best. Frankie had never faced a problem she couldn't solve with inventing. She said good-bye to Maya and moped her way home.

When she got home, she flopped onto the couch. She felt like she was a pancake on the road that had been run over by an eighteen-wheeler.

She had built the trap. She had tested the trap. She had thought about all the ways it could fail. And she still couldn't prove whether leprechauns existed.

"How's my favorite inventor?"

Frankie looked up. She was surprised to see her aunt Nichelle standing in the doorway of the living room. "Aunt Nichelle! What are you doing here?"

"I wanted to see how the leprechaun experiments were going," she said. She sat down gently next to Frankie.

"Not so good," Frankie said. "I built the best trap I could, but it didn't catch the leprechaun. I thought that was what I wanted, since it would prove they didn't exist. But maybe there aren't any leprechauns around here. Or maybe there is one and it just didn't happen upon my trap. It's hopeless!"

"Whoa," Aunt Nichelle said. "Slow down."

Frankie took a deep breath.

"What did Newton say?" Aunt Nichelle asked.

Frankie sniffled. "'If I have seen further, it is by standing upon the shoulders of giants.'" It was kind of a family motto.

"Right," Aunt Nichelle said. "Without Darwin, your aunt Gina wouldn't be able to understand rodents. Without Grace Hopper, your mom wouldn't be able to do her work with robots. Without Henry Ford, Uncle Irwin wouldn't be able to design those race cars. And without numerous scientists and astronauts, I couldn't do my work."

"I know," Frankie said. She wasn't sure how this was supposed to make her feel better.

"Well, those people were the pioneers," Aunt Nichelle said. "Just like you."

Frankie looked up at her aunt with just a hint of hope in her heart. "What do you mean?" she asked.

"Frankie, I don't know of anyone else who has brought serious science to the idea of leprechauns. You are a pioneer. And sure, maybe you didn't find the answers you were looking for, but you laid the groundwork."

Frankie sniffed again. "You mean it?"

"I do." Aunt Nichelle picked up Frankie's trap. "This is really impressive, Frankie. You should be very proud of yourself. I mean, the next person who wants to study leprechauns should definitely start with this trap. You've thought of everything."

Frankie smiled, and Aunt Nichelle gave her a kiss on the top of her head.

"Wait, Aunt Nichelle. How will people know about my trap?"

"That's the last step of the design process, Frankie. You know that."

Aunt Nichelle was right. Frankie did know that. And she knew what she needed to do next.

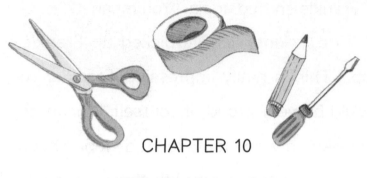

CHAPTER 10

Wonder On

FRANKIE AND MAYA WENT INTO THE school library the next day and said good morning to Ms. Appleton.

"Good morning, girls!" Ms. Appleton said. "How are two of my favorite wonderers?"

"Awesome," Maya said.

"Splendiferous," Frankie agreed. She handed Ms. Appleton the index card she had worked on the evening before. Aunt Nichelle

had read it over and helped her fix the spelling mistakes, but all the ideas had been Frankie's.

"Another 'I wonder' solved?" Ms. Appleton asked.

"Not exactly," Frankie said.

Ms. Appleton looked at the card. She read it aloud.

"ARE LEPRECHAUNS REAL? THAT IS A TOUGH QUESTION! TO FIND OUT, I CREATED A SCIENTIFIC EXPERIMENT. MY GOAL WAS TO SEE IF I COULD CATCH A LEPRECHAUN. IF I DID, THEN OBVIOUSLY WE WOULD KNOW THAT LEPRECHAUNS DO EXIST. IF I DIDN'T, I THOUGHT THAT MEANT WE WOULD KNOW THAT THEY DIDN'T EXIST. BUT LEPRECHAUNS AREN'T THAT SIMPLE. WE DIDN'T CATCH A LEPRECHAUN, AND AT FIRST I THOUGHT THAT MEANT I'D PROVED THAT LEPRECHAUNS DIDN'T EXIST. BUT THEN MAYA POINTED OUT THAT MAYBE IT JUST MEANT THAT NO LEPRECHAUNS HAD COME TO THE

TRAP. I THOUGHT MY EXPERIMENT WAS A FAILURE. THEN I REALIZED THAT MY RESEARCH WAS JUST A STARTING POINT. IT RAISED SOME GOOD QUESTIONS, LIKE, 'WHAT IS THE BEST BAIT FOR LEPRE-CHAUNS?' AND 'DO LEPRECHAUNS HIBERNATE?'

"SOMETIMES EXPERIMENTS ANSWER QUESTIONS. SOMETIMES THEY JUST RAISE MORE QUESTIONS. AT FIRST THAT WAS FRUSTRATING TO ME. NOW I HOPE THAT IF ANYONE ELSE WONDERS ABOUT LEPRECHAUNS, THEY WILL USE MY EXPERIMENTS TO HELP THEM ASK QUESTIONS AND FIND ANSWERS."

Ms. Appleton lowered the card and looked at Frankie. "Frankie, I am very impressed. I know you like to have answers to your question."

"I do," Frankie said. "But sometimes it's nice to wonder."

"It is, isn't it?" Ms. Appleton said.

Maya smiled. "Wonder on, Ms. Appleton," she said.

"Wonder on, girls," Ms. Appleton replied.

Frankie and Maya hooked elbows and walked down the hallway toward Ms. Cupid's room.

"I've been thinking about your Opus problem," Frankie said.

"My Opus problem?" Maya replied.

"With the hoop. Leprechauns are mysterious, but we know a lot about Opus. He likes going into boxes, and onto the couch, right?"

"That's true," Maya agreed.

"Maybe he likes squares better than round things," Frankie said. "Or maybe a different-color hoop? Or one that smells like bacon? Or—"

"Oh, Frankie!" Maya said. "You never stop, do you?"

"Nope!" Frankie said.

"Good," Maya told her. "Because I've got a lot of things I wonder about."

Frankie smiled. Whatever Maya wondered about, Frankie was sure she could find a way to investigate. Maybe she wouldn't find all the answers, but she could certainly get the ball rolling.

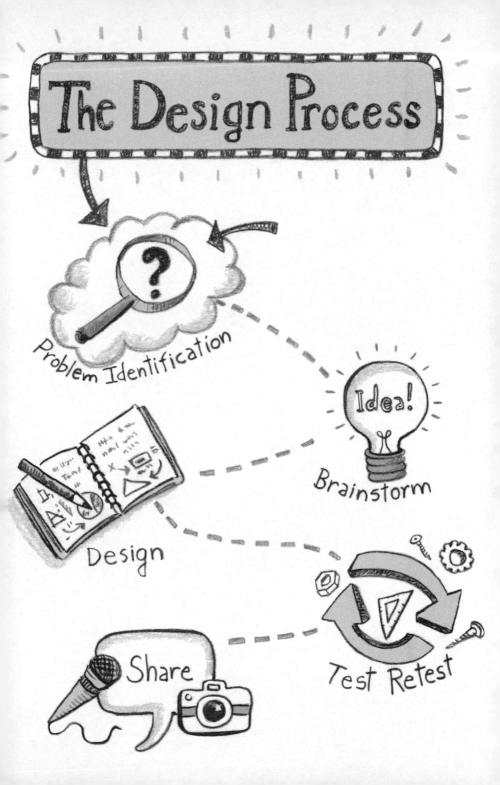

Anticipating
Failure

IN THIS STORY FRANKIE LEARNS THAT
engineers try to guess how their designs might
fail. Testing and retesting is part of the design
process, and failure testing extends that idea
to imagine failures that *might* happen, even if
they don't show up in the testing.

Frankie makes a list of all the ways her trap
could fail and then tries to solve each of those

problems. For example, adding layers of plastic and sand to the trap would make it harder for a leprechaun to get out. She also adds the fail-safe of glitter so that even if, against all odds, her trap fails, she will have evidence of a leprechaun having been there.

This is what we mean by "failure testing." This step is important, because testing may not expose all of the faults in an invention. Frankie's aunt Nichelle is working on a project for a garden in space. Going to space costs a lot of money, so she can't run all her experiments up in space. She needs to be able to do some of them on the ground. By anticipating failure, she is finding ways to make her design as good as possible before sending it into orbit.

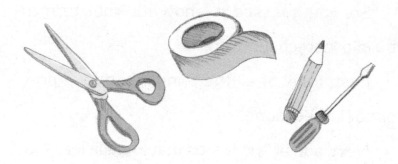

What Could Possibly
Go Wrong?

IN THIS STORY FRANKIE HAS TO THINK about all the ways her leprechaun trap might not work. She also does some research about leprechauns, both in books and through her experiments with the trap. As her aunt Nichelle tells her, sometimes the first person to investigate a problem doesn't solve it. That person sets a foundation for others to build upon.

So, you guessed it—now it's your turn to build a leprechaun trap!

First, think of all the things that you know about leprechauns.

Next, add all the things that Frankie learned.

Then go to the library and see if you can find out any more information about leprechauns.

With this information in mind, design and build your leprechaun trap.

Now it's time for the fun part: failure!

Try to think of all the ways your trap could fail. Ask yourself, "What could possibly go wrong?" Make a list. Then ask yourself, "How could I stop that failure from happening?" You could use a table like this:

Possible Problem	My Solution

When your trap is done, put it out some-where in your home and see what you catch.

Keep careful records. Together we may be able to prove once and for all whether lepre-chauns exist!

Acknowledgments

Thank you to the terrific team at Aladdin who help to bring Frankie Sparks into the world, especially editor Alyson Heller, copyeditor Karen Sherman, cover designer Laura Lyn DiSiena, and interior designers Mike Rosamilia and Tiara Iandiorio. Thank you to Nadja Sarell, whose illustrations of Frankie, her inventions, and her friends are joyful and full of life.

Thank you to my agent, Sara Crowe, for always supporting me.

Thank you to my family, especially to

Matilda and Jack, who allowed me to study their leprechaun-trap-making process.

Thanks to all the teachers, librarians, and other educators who are designing and inventing with their students.

And a big, big thanks to all the readers who have contacted me to let me know how much they enjoy reading about Frankie Sparks!

Don't miss Frankie's first invention!

FRANKIE SPARKS HAD A STORY TO share. It was the best story ever. It gurgled in her stomach as she rode the bus to school. It fizzed in her fingers and toes when she and Suki Moskovitz and Maya played Don't Touch the Hot Lava on the playground before school. It threatened to pop out of her mouth like a burp while they put their things away in their cubbies and did their morning work. But she managed to hold on to it all the way until morning meeting. By then she could barely contain herself.

Frankie was in third grade at Grace Hopper Elementary, which was the luckiest place to go to school. Plus she had the best teacher, Ms. Cupid. And her best friend in the whole world, Maya, was in her class, and Ms. Cupid even let them be partners 50 percent of the time.

Every Monday at morning meeting Ms. Cupid asked her class to share what they had done over the weekend. So, as soon as Frankie and her twenty classmates crowded down on the rug, Frankie raised her hand as high as she could. She stretched up on her knees and wiggled her fingers. But she didn't say anything. Not one word. Her teacher, Ms. Cupid, did not like it when kids blurted.

Ms. Cupid called on Lila Jones, who played with her shoelaces while she launched into a long story about her soccer game and how it had rained and how they had sat in their cars until the rain ended. Then they got to play the game, and Lila claimed they had won 3–2, but then Suki, who was on the team too, said, no, they had tied 3–3. *How could you not even know if you had won or tied the game?* Frankie wondered.

"What matters is that you both played very hard, I'm sure," Ms. Cupid said. "And were good sports about it."

Frankie thought that of course it mattered that they had played hard and were good sports, but it also mattered who had won or lost. It was a game, after all. "You really can't remember if you won or tied?" she asked.

"Frankie," Ms. Cupid warned. "We're moving on."

So Frankie shot her hand up into the air again. Ms. Cupid called on Luke Winslow, who talked about *his* soccer game. At least he knew who'd won—the other team—but he still went on and on and on.

When Luke was done, Frankie shot her hand into the air again, and finally Ms. Cupid called on her.

"We went to see my aunt at the university where she works. She's a rodentologist. And—"

"Excuse me, Frankie. I'm sorry to interrupt, but I think some of our friends might not know what a rodentologist is."

"It's someone who studies rodents. We got to see mice and hamsters and white rats and . . ." Frankie took a deep breath. This was the best part of her story. "A capybara." She pronounced the word slowly, just the way her aunt had taught her: *cap-ah-bear-ah*.

"It's like a guinea pig, but it's four feet long!" Frankie rocked forward. "I got to lie down next to it. It was longer than me!"

Capybara
Hydrochaerus hydrochaeris

"Cool!" Luke exclaimed.

Lila wrinkled her nose, but Suki said, "Wow!" Suki almost never said "Wow!" It was usually reserved for things like back handsprings and T-shirts with glitter on them.

And of course Maya, Frankie's best friend in the whole wide world, gave Frankie a big grin.

"That is so cool, Frankie," Ms. Cupid agreed. And then she flipped over the page with the morning message on it and wrote down the word "rodentologist" on the blank piece of chart paper below. She tapped her pointer against the word. "What a great vocabulary word." Underneath it she wrote, *Biologist.* She explained, "A biologist is someone who studies living things. A rodentologist is a type of biologist. They study rodents like mice and rats. Can anyone think of any other types of biologists?"

Frankie put her hand up. She knew all kinds of biologists. Ms. Cupid called on Luke, who said, "A bugologist?"

"Great!" Ms. Cupid said. Frankie was pretty sure that "great" was Ms. Cupid's favorite word. She used it all the time. "A biologist who studies insects is called an entomologist." She wrote that word down on the chart paper in her neat, straight print. "Anyone else?"

"Maybe a herpetologist?" Ravi asked. He didn't even stumble over the big word.

"Yes!" Ms. Cupid cheered. "And what's a herpetologist?"

"Someone who studies lizards and amphibians."

Suki asked, "How about someone who studies fish?"

"Oh! Terrific, Suki! This is actually one of my all-time top-ten favorite words. *Ichthyologist.* Can everyone say that?"

The class stumbled over the word as they tried to say it back to her. "We'll work on it. We have plenty of time." She put down her pointer and looked right at Frankie. "I'm so glad you shared this today, because it's just perfect for something we are going to do later. I was going to tell you after snack, but I think I'll spill my secret now." She smiled, and the silver in her braces sparkled. Frankie hadn't even known that grown-ups could have braces, but Ms. Cupid did, and Frankie thought they were as beautiful on her teeth as any jewelry.